CHICAGO BLUES

A Murder Mystery Crime
Suspense Thriller

by

Saul Tillock

CONTENTS

WHAT THE CRITICS SAID

"Tillock has singlehandedly created a new genre: Illiterature." Liam Walker, *Tipperary Tribune*

"A real page-burner" Andrea Swanson, *West Boston Book Review*

"Egregious" Manly Tusk, *The Essex Observer*

"Bestsellers aren't meant to be this good. They're meant to be much, much better." Nic Lender, *The View*

"I couldn't put it down, because I wouldn't pick it up." Brioin O'Brioin, *The Literary Supplement*

"Books like this only come along once in a generation – thank God." Layla Tyler, *Hoopers' Weekly*

"In a world of average writers, Tillock stands head and shoulders below them all" Amy Twee, *The Guide*

CHAPTER 1

The Shadowy Shadow

A howly type of a wind was blowing like mad through the calm still air of Chicago Town, in America, the States. Goldy rays of silver sunlight bounced reflectively off the shiny blue ripples on top of the water in the lakes, ponds, canals and other various water features all over Chicago Town, America, The States. In one particular place, to be specific, a couple was walking along the street on an otherwise empty boulevard. Otherwise empty, that is, except for them. They were Jake Fritter and Amy Gladly, if that was her real name.

Tall, attractive handsome Jake Fritter, who was really really good-looking with high cheekbones and everything like a male model even though he wasn't one cos he was an undercover private detective, was leading the amazingly sexy long-legged, nice-faced lovely-haired Amy Gladly, if that was her real name, by one of her two hands, towards his high-classed ultra-expensive beachfront condo in the centre of Chicago Town.

Chicago Town, city of hope, fear, anger, joy, and courage, and 2.736 million people, each of them with a story to tell; 17 stories some of them, others only 2. So if we say on average 11 stories, we're talking roughly 30 million stories. 31 million tops. And this was theirs (Jake and Amy's).

"Come on in." Jake said in his deep, manly Chicago drawl,

at the main door of his apartment block, and she said ok and she did and they went in. They had had had enough of the Windy City, its jazz music, its famous museum of science and history, its proximity to the great lakes, and its high crime stats (short for statistics). They had just met in a bar just round the corner, and just liked each other immediately cos they were both just looking for someone just like that. He had backed into her front while looking the other way and spilt her drink and bought her another one. That's how they met.

"Thank you for the prompt replacement of the drink you spilt", she said.

"You're welcome" he said, transfixed by her eyes, which were beautiful and kind. Both eyes were both, that is. She didn't have one kind eye and one beautiful one. Each eye was both beautiful *and* kind.

She said "What do you do?" and he said "I'm a private detective, but don't tell anyone, it's private ha ha." She laughed as well, cos she appreciated a man who knew how to laugh at his own jokes that was really really good-looking like him. Jake also liked how *she* laughed, throwing her beautiful happy face upwards and bellowing like a bull who's just got a bull-joke. He showed her his private eye ID and she showed him her novelty mallet she'd just bought in a novelty shop and they laughed again.

He didn't tell her that when he bumped into her by accident he was actually on a private-eye case, and he had had had his private eye on someone in particular, a man with a limp in one of his legs, who had come into the bar just minutes before. Jake didn't want to lose the limpy fella in the crowd, but also didn't want *him* to know *he* was following *him*, so using *his* private eye training (which *he* had learned from youTube tutorials), *he* had casually rushed in backwards, and backed right into Amy's front, and spilt and replaced her drink.

He also didn't tell her that while she was busy giggling and guffawing, he had surreptitiously turned around to resume keeping his private eye on his target, and saw he was all-of-a-sudden gone. Jake just kept acting all casual like nothing had happened cos he was undercover, and being visibly agitated or overtly aghast would've blown his undercover right off, making people think "Hang on, who's this oddball with the untoward antics?" Anyway he was having more fun with Amy now than being on the case now anyway so he didn't care. They hit it off with each other immediately cos they both fancied each other.

As they entered his condo apartment entrance, Amy still laughing at his brash boisterous barrage of bawdy anecdotes, Jake also didn't tell her one more thing. He didn't just want *her* to see the inside of his apartment, *he* wanted to see the inside of *her* clothes too, and not just because he liked her clothes, which were full of fashion, oozing snazz and swank. He knew from what he'd already seen of her hands, feet, elbows and face, that he'd probably like the rest of her too. And having got to know her a bit, he knew, deep down, in his heart of hearts, if he were to be completely honest on an emotional level, he'd really like to see her whole body in the actual nude.

Finally, they were inside his luxury condo. Gradually she settled down, still tittering and gurgling a bit, like when you try and stop laughing but you can't and it keeps coming out in little chuckle-puffs, or chuffs.

They conversed good-naturedly and had a few drinks, not each, come on, they weren't alchoes, but between them. Mind you, they knocked back a fair bit, probably gin, or whiskey, who knows? Anyway, before long, they were buckled; as buckled as a bag of belts, secured with a large bag-buckle.

He served her from his own home bar which he had had had put in his front room by a fella who seemed nice at the time but charged way too much and he had had had to bargain him down, but he didn't get much off, which still annoyed him a bit, and he couldn't really give Amy's chitchat his full attention while he thought about how *annoying* that'd been.

After a while, during a gap in her babbling when she had had had to inhale, he quickly suggested that they go upstairs, as it would be higher up and therefore safer in the event of a flood. She agreed and they climbed up the stairs calmly in single file.

No sooner had they opened and shut the bedroom door than they were in the bedroom. The room itself was nice, and furnished tastefully with furnishings, of a deep rich colour. In the middle of the room, the bed beckoned. Not literally, but in a kind of a way.

Excitement rose up through their eager insides like bubbles in any number of fizzy drinks brands, for example. Overwhelmed with an all-consuming passion, they couldn't help themselves, or anyone else. They chitted and chatted about this and that for approximately 9 seconds, and then, throwing all pretense aside (probably to the left) they pushed each other onto the bed, (not at the same time, as Newton's third law would have made their equally opposing forces cancel out, but by taking multiple mini-turns, each pushing the other incrementally in the same direction, towards the bed).

What followed was really explicit and raunchy, and they were both so fit from eating nutritionally and going to the gym, that they were able to go for ages, so they went at it like a set of hammers and tongs (if you imagine people-shaped ones on a bed) till they were finished.

Afterwards, it was over, and they didn't do it any more, cos they couldn't, even though they were really fit; *that's* how much they'd gone for it.

Suddenly, Jake noticed a slight movement downstairs, outside, behind the back wall on the other side of the house. Don't ask how. He could just kind of sense it; he had like a fifth sense. Up and out like a flash, he ran down the stairs thinking, "Lucky I know how to get dressed really quick after sex so I can go and deal with stuff that I sense."

At the bottom of the stairs he was downstairs, and he made his way warily like a cat (probably a large domestic tabby), to the back window at the back of the house. It wasn't really a window, more kind of them glass doors that slide, whatever they're called, slidey window doors? He thought he could see a shadowy form outside, a shadowy form whose shadow was reflected on the roller blinds (which were down by the way, in case you're trying to picture all this in your imagination. There was a brown mat on the floor if that's any help).

Carefully, he started pulling on the beady chain-type thing that makes the blinds go up, but he was pulling it the wrong way, and he had to stop and go back the other way. Then, he started sliding open the slidey window doors, cautiously at first, but that was taking ages, so eventually he just flung them open, and jumped outside in the prepared-to-fight position.

The sun was really really shiny and it could have blinded him, but luckily there was a thick layer of cloud under it, so it was dull and dark out, you could hardly even tell it was daytime. Suddenly, just as he looked round, before he could do anything, he heard a kind of squeak, and a huge punch landed (BAM!) on the back of his head.

"Ow, what you do that for!?!" he said, but he was unconscious before he even said it. Then everything went black, blacker than a black horse with no teeth or eyes on a moonless night.

CHAPTER 2

The Ex

J ake woke up in hospital, or to be more precise, in a hospital bed. His ex-girlfriend Sarah, a top fashion model who had stridden catwalks from Paris to you name it, was sitting beside his bedside, holding his hand in one of her own two hands, probably her left one, as she was sitting on his right, so that hand would have been the handiest for holding

"Hiya Jake!" she tootled chirpily

"Hi Sarah, what happened me?" he said in his deep gravel-topped Chicago drawl.

"You were battered by an intruder" she said.

"Wow, heavy" he said.

"I know" she said, "in this day and age!"

"What about Amy?"

"Amy?" She said back to him

"Yes, Amy my beautiful sexy recent friend that I plan to make into my full-on girlfriend and life-partner, who was with me when the events described up to this point occurred?" he elaborated

"Well," Sarah responded "there was no sign of anyone else in the apartment when police-cops arrived on the scene after noticing the blinds were drawn slightly differently than usual while on a routine patrol in the area and decided to investigate further."

"Oh. I hope she's alright." Jake began, inconsolably worried. "Anyhoo. So, Sarah, how come you're here?" he continued, beginning to take in his surroundings which was a hospitalroom with all the stuff that goes in them, and eventually focusing on Sarah's supple undulating curves, which were all in the right places, (he presumed, some curves were round the back where he couldn't see), and remembering some steamy sex times the two of them had had had when they had been a thing.

"The hospital staff people called me; you still have me listed as your next-off-kin in your wallet's documentation flap." She explained.

"How have you been anyway?" he blurt-asked caringly.

She started to tell him, all stuff about her family and people she'd met, college courses she'd started, a romance that floundered, and this and that, but he stopped listening after a while cos he couldn't help wondering about what had happened to *him*.

"Do the police-cops have any idea who did it?" He wandered out aloud abruptly, interrupting her going on about herself.

"There was no signs of a break-in or a struggle." She replied. "The matter is being looked into by the authorities and at this time foul play is not suspected. However, police-cops are not ruling out a co-ordinated terrorist attack, a minor domestic accident, or institutionalized medical malpractice." She intoned, suggestively.

"Hmm, someone's not telling somebody something" said Jake quietly, though loud enough for Sarah to hear him, cos the room was pin-drop quiet cos mobile phones have to be off or else on silent (ie where they just kind of buzz) in hospitals, otherwise it interferes with medical machines and people die.

"What do you mean?" Sarah probed curiously

"I think there's some kind of coverup," began Jake "for who or whom or whome I don't know, but I smell corruption," he continued, "It smells kind of vinegary with a hint of coriander; and I got a feeling it goes all the way to the top." he finished

"...to the top...?"" Sarah gasped unbelievably "You mean...

God?!?"

"Well, no ... maybe not that far, but certainly to the higher etchelons of the government, and possibly the UN, the IMF, and World Bank." Jake reassured her, and proceeded to fill her in, (without mentioning any names, just using initials, for her own safety) on how he'd been hired on the phone by H.M. a shady megalomaniac type, to track down Nefertiti's Eye, a huge sapphire said to be worth priceless billions, which had recently been stolen from the Chicago Museum by H.M's nemesis, D.S. who had a limp in one of his legs. He'd been closing in on D.S too, when he met Amy Gladly, if that was her real name, and got all distracted.

"What's that got to do with the UN and the World Bank and all that though?" said Sarah, but Jake ignored her, becoming surly and dismissive.

"Be like that then" she snarled understandingly, "see if I care."

He didn't care if she cared or not. Exhausted, he sank back into his pillow like a ship sinking into a pillow with all hands on deck, if you can drown hands. He couldn't help wondering: (1) Who was trying to kill him, (2) Who wanted him dead? (3) Why go to all the trouble of murdering him, why not just ask him to go away? (He always responded well to politeness) and (3a) Why *hadn't* they killed him?

So many questions, and so many answers. But right now, all he had was the questions.

"Well well", Jake whispered quietly inside his inner mind "This mystery is getting even more mysteriouser than what it already was", and then he nodded off.

CHAPTER 3

Young Jake

Jake hadn't always been a private dick (detective in other words). When he was a kid, back in his younger childhood days, he didn't know *what* he wanted to be.

One day he thought he'd like to be a train driver, hurtling between mountains, head out the window roaring into the wind, while inside the train, the rest of his body shovelled coal into a rumbling furnace.

The next day, he'd picture himself as a gnarled squinting watchmaker, sitting in oaky ticking silence, tutting at tooth-wheeled intricacies and fiddling with bits of springs. The next he'd be a taut, fakely grinning ballet dancer, wincing silently under the weight of a ballerina prancing across his rigid frame to the music they have in those things.

And the next, a rugged zookeeper, clanking gates, flinging raw steak to tigers and scooping up hippo-shit; or a crouched, beardy chess champion, or a giant dwarf; though Jake knew how to do none of these things. That's kids for you.

Growing up in Milwaukee, 92.6 miles (149km) north of Chicago on the shores of Lake Michigan, among a population of 595,348 other Milwaukens, young Jake Fritter, the middle Fritter of 3, (between his older brother and younger sister), was pretty undecided about pretty much everything. And not just in the long term, even in the daily now-times. He refused to enter any debates with his vociferous siblings, proclaiming "my opinions are nascent, I can contribute nothing to this discussion".

It was as if he was saving himself for his true calling, even though that was albeit as yet still unknown. All through school and/or college he refused to commit to any profession, exasperating his parents, teachers, several career guidance counsellors, and Len, the local astronaut (who went to space to get away from his parents, who wanted him to be a weightlifter, like them).

Then, one day, while Jake was sitting around unemployed in his mid-twenties up in his room still living at home with his parents shaving while watching telly in the mirror in Milwaukee not knowing what to do with himself, he saw an episode of The Rockford Files. All of a sudden he *knew* that was what he wanted to do. (Be a detective, not be on telly.)

His first few cases were fairly run of the mill, missing pets, extra-marital affairs, that sorts of things, but then he solved a major murder, and he was in demand.

Then he hit the bottle and lost most of his clients, but then he cleaned up his act and started over, but with smaller cases again, parking violations, internet security breaches, lost toys etc.

That's when notorious Morroco-based Chicago-born super-crook and businessman, Hector Maltoward (H.M) rang him up and hired him to follow Chicago-born-and-still-based-in-Chicago-mega-crook, Devon Starbood (D.S).

Jake didn't like taking crooked money to do crooked stuff, but like his dad used to say, "Money is money is money", and money or not, this was money, and he needed money cos he had no money.

With the first bit of money he got, he rented his condo. Then, while earning his next bit of money, he spilt the drink and met Amy Gladly, if that was her real name.

CHAPTER 4

Catastrophic Cataclysm

Meanwhile, back in the now-times, Jake was awake again, still groggy, but staggering around in a coherent daze, helped by Sarah, his gorgeous ex, who he still really fancied but who(m?) had dumped him several months ago, (for a guy who then dumped *her* cos he thought she was too clingy, but she wasn't, she just kept grabbing on to him cos he lived on a slope and she was worried she'd fall over).

She was trying to get Jake to get back into his hospital bed and get some sleep and get better, but get-back-into-bed-and-get-some-sleep-and-get-better he would *not*.

"No Sarah", he said "I've got a mystery to solve, a case to catch up on, and a city to serve, the streets aren't safe without me out there".

"Don't be silly." says Sarah, closing the sort of little window in the top part of the normal window, which is also a window in it's own right (you know the ones, with a handle of their own and everything) to block out the incessant honking hootage of the mid-afternoon Chicago Town traffic.

"Sarah, I'll say it once, and I can't unsay it, there isn't a street out there that won't be unsafe without my absence."

Sarah thought about this.

"Yes there is," she said finally, "I think." and she pulled down the blinds and tucked him firmly back into his bunk, drawing herself up to her full 5 ft 13 inch sexy supermodel height. He remembered what he'd always liked about her, "a certain…je ne say quoi" or as the French say, "I dunno what".

This brief french-talky reverie was interrupted by another, more sinister cogitation. Could it be, he suddenly wondered, things starting to fall into place now that he had had had a nap and had had had time to mull things over, could it be that H.M had for some reason changed his mind about his nemesis, D.S, done a deal with him behind Jake's back, and, rather than telling Jake, was now trying to have him killed to cover his tracks?

'Huh! Can't trust anyone these days', Jake thought pensively. He looked at Sarah, who had conveniently turned up out of the blue, and wondered if he could even trust *her*. They had history, sure, but so did most history books, and they often turn out to be untrustworthy when contrasted with rigorous historical research done under laboratory conditions.

What if she was part of H.M's scheme to murder him, or what if D.S had hired her to do the same? What if they were *both* trying to kill him? Had Chicago's two most powerful deadly criminals joined up and turned their combined powerful deadlinesses on him, via Sarah? Well, had they? Hmm?

He pondered all about it while he gazed at her with sleepy suspicion. Slowly, methodically, his mind weighed everything up, and by following cold hard logic step by step, he came to the inescapable conclusion that Sarah looked too beautiful to be tainted by the ugliness of evil.

"Now you stay in that bed" Sarah said mock-menacingly, cheerfully unaware of his slowly subsiding suspicions and diminishing doubts "or I'll have to slap some sense into you." She showed him the back of her extremely large left hand for emphasis. Even if he managed to overpower *that* hand, he reasoned, she probably had another in reserve, just as big. It was pointless fighting, he thought, and went back to sleep.

Jake Fritter was like that, he could sleep anywhere if he really concentrated and tried hard and put his mind to it. It usually took about an hour, maybe two, two and a half tops.

His mum said once, "Jake Fritter, if you were dropped in a volcano and there was a bed there, you'd eventually go straight to sleep, and you wouldn't even wake up even if it erupted in a catastrophic cataclysm like Krakatoa in August of 1863, ejecting an ash plume over 6.2km high, at the cost of over 36,000 lives!" He didn't realise how right she was at the time, as he was only a few weeks old, but one day those words would come back to haunt him, like the word "Boo".

As soon as he begun to snore, Sarah grabs the end of his bunk and goes reversing backwards, wheeling him out through the corridors and loads of those flappy doors.

On the way she back-bashes into a weirdly smiling doctor coming the other way with a big needle-syringe who she doesn't trust there's just *something about him* and BAM! the momentum of her shoulder hits him in his part of your chest where your ribs all join up together, and he falls on the needle-syringe and injects himself in the part of your eye you look out of with a lethal dose of hydrogen pentaxodrol which kills him after an agonising bout of writhing, twitching and spewing yellow froth out of his mouth and anus, but Sarah doesn't see any of this cos she's already out in the car park loading the still-asleep-gently-snoring-unconscious-dreaming Jake into the back seat of her Mitsubishi Lancer.

CHAPTER 5

Elbows

While he was asleep in Sarah's car, Jake drempt he was up a tree, which was great, cos he loved being up trees, but then the tree started licking itself like a cat, and he fell into a massive food-mixer. It wasn't on or anything, don't worry!

He got on well with most of the food and they became close friends in a relationship based on trust, but then a huge hand like Sarah's (not her actual hand, cos it was just a dream), came down as if to switch on the mixer. It was a terrifying moment, so terrifying it woke him up.

He slowly realised he wasn't in hospital any more but in the back seat of Sarah's 2 litre front-wheel drive fully automatic fuel-efficient Mitsubishi Lancer, and she was going round and round and round a roundabout, if they have them in America. She had had had a dizzy spell going round and round and round the roundabout and now she didn't know where to get off.

"I was having this mad crazy dream" he said. "I was up a-"

"I don't care, all dreams are bollocks" she interjected curtly, "just random shit your brain spews out when you're asleep."

"Oh." He said, bemused and beflated. He looked at the countryside spinning around outside the car, all blurry, flying past the window like loads of food in a food mixer, if the food looked like trees and hedges. Maybe broccoli and cress?

"Where are we?" he said

"We're halfway between kind of, and completely, lost" she said, laughing dizzily, nostrils flaring with roundabout-rage, lips distended, and her eyes yearning for something intangible.

"Don't you have a sat-naval machine?" he said "or googly maps or anything?"

"No", she said, "I don't believe in them, I'm self-sufficient, have been since I was two." She began to fondly recount her first faltering attempts at self-sufficiency as a toddler, when she had begun dressing her own salads, knitting her own mittens, and generally living off the land.

As nostalgia clouded her road-perception, she sliced through three lanes of traffic, and it was only lucky she drove through the gaps between vehicles that all the other people including her on the roundabout wasn't dead. She wrestled control of the fuel efficient Mitsubishi Lancer back just in time to keep it on the road after they emerged on an exit lane. "Anyway I'm sure your house isn't far from here…" she said

'Hang on, how does she even know where I live?' Jake thought privately to himself in a tiny inside voice. He had had had a different apartment when they'd been a thing, not his *new* pad. It just didn't make sense, hold water, stack right, stack left, or add up.

She was trying to pull the wool over his eyes and he didn't like it. One thing he detested was wool-pulling of the over-eye variety. It was obvious, she was now working for someone or maybe more than one someones, who wanted him *DEAD*.

No, she couldn't be, not Sarah, she was on his side, he'd proven empirically in his mind that she was too pretty to be evil. But what if she was ugly on the *inside?* But isn't everyone, with all those guts and yucky gunk?

His mind kept pulling him this way and that in two different directions like two warlike teams of people tugging a rope in opposite directions.

"But I haven't a clue where you live these days, so we'll just go to my place" she continued.

Jake palpated with palpable relief, and thought badly of himself for having thought so badly of her. He remembered fondly where her place was, not far from here. But she was taking ages, so in a surprise move, Jake grabbed her elbows from behind and that way he could kind of drive using her arms, and eventually they got to her place.

Sarah exploded (in a kind of a way) when they got out.

"You didn't have to hold my elbows!"

"Sorry", he said, "but time is of the essens. I need to work out who's trying to kill me, find the missing woman I was with, gauge general safety levels in the area, and attend to several other pressing matters"

When they got inside, the place was a bit of a mess, so he helped her tidy up for a few hours. He Hoovered with the Dyson and then they watched some ads she had had had recorded (her telly-box could be set to record just the ads, so you didn't have to watch the annoying programs in between). Then they had some pizza in her living room.

The air was filled with a tangible sense of sexual tension that you could touch with your hand, they could both feel it emanating out of each other, but they didn't say anything about it or refer to it in any way. Jake scrolled through his phone messages but there was none from Amy.

Finally, more than a little impatiently, i.e. normal-sized impatiently, Sarah said "Well come on then, what are we waiting for? Let's go and solve your mystery."

"Alright, keep your nose on!" Jake blurted, all tired and emotional from all the stress and tension he'd been traumatised by and was still struggling with lately.

"Sorry, I thought you were in a hurry with who's trying to kill you and where's Amy and the general level of street safety and all that." She inferred.

"I am, but we don't want *them* to know that." He said pointedly

"Who's *them*?" she asked bluntly

21

"The *others*, the ones who could be behind all this, who might be listening" he said, onimously

"I think we might be too late for that", she said, even more onimously, looking outside through the window.

CHAPTER 6

Maltoward

Meanwhile, several thousand miles away (maybe slightly less), on the balcony of a luxury hotel in Marrakesh in Morocco in Africa, H.M. aka Hector Maltoward, a man who looked like a giant toad, or a frog with warts, or a swarthy salamander, certainly something amphibious anyway, was sitting in his white flannel suit, sipping a cool green créme de menthe, and looking abstractively out over the gold-plated balcony of his hotel-room at Miranda.

Miranda, his amazingly sexy fifth wife (or as he called her, his amazingly filthy sex wife) was splashing around and giggling in the hotel's luxury high-classed swimming pool, which was kidney-bean shaped (but not sized, or coloured). The hot African Moroccan Marrakesh sun blazed shinily down on his wide-brimmed-type of straw hat (you know the ones), and the thick yellowy-white smoke from his cigar drifted silently around the brim of it like a smoky yellowy-white brim-cloud type smoke ring.

"Hector!" giggled Miranda, "you *simply must* come in, the water's terribly, awfully, absolutely divine!"

He smiled, raising his sun-sparkled green glass to her. Looking at her through it, she looked all green and bendy and mad-looking.

"I'm busy, woman" (he could never remember their names).

"Besides, you look like you're having quite enough fun on your own without me by yourself."

It was true, Miranda just loved water, it never ceased to amaze, thrill and exhilarate her. Puddles, ponds, pools and ports, lakes, rivers and mugs, she just couldn't get enough of the amazing wet liquid that filled them all.

Hector Maltoward went back to working on his MacBook Pro, which is one of the best MacBooks you can get, mainly meant for professionals, hence the "Pro". This one had over a hundred thousand gigabytes of hard drive, 932gb ram, a 98.2 ghz processor, a really high resolution screen, and a highly intuitive (i.e. easy-to use) operating system. The only thing it didn't have was power. He'd forgot to get one of those power adaptor plug thingies for when you're abroad. So he was just using it to lean on while he wrote poetry, but it was still his favourite computer by a mile (1.6km).

As he wrote, he occasionally gazed for inspiration into the vast Moroccan distance, where he could see, across the Sahara, the triangly tops of the pyramids, built years ago by the beautiful but deadly Cleopatra, queen of the Zulus, to damm the Amazon, Africa's mightiest river. But no inspiration had came so far, so so far, his poem had only three lines:

There once was a man from Uganda,
Who had an affair with a panda,
It made him quite itchy-

He had just thought of a rhyme for "itchy" when his phone rang:

Briiiing briiing, briiiiiiing briiing, briiing, briiiiiiing briiing, briiing, briiiiiiing briiing, briiing, briiiiiiing briiing, briiing, briiiiiiing briiing, briiing, briiiii-

He picked it up and said what. It was Trev, his trusty underling, who was at that very moment doing his bidding (Hector's that is, not his own) on the other side of the world.

"Hello sir"

"Ah," said Hector with jovial conviviality (not to be confused with convivial joviality, a form of intense twitching)

"How's things Trev?"

"I'd prefer *agent X* if you don't mind, sir, seeing as we're on the phone and all that"

"Well?" said Maltoward, asking the one-word open-ended single-syllabled four-lettered question all his minions dreaded.

"I've found him, boss", says Trev. There was a silence of about 4 seconds at the other end of the line, as Hector thought about this. When he'd finished thinking, he let the silence linger for a further 3 seconds, as he felt longer lingering silences made him seem more sinister, and he preferred a total linger-length of 7 seconds.

"Who, Jake Fritter?" Hector broke the silence into two roughly equal parts with his exclamation.

"*The Target* sir, if you don't mind"

"Where?" said Hector

"Chicago Town." Trev says

"Chicago Town?" Hector said

"Yeah, it's in the middle of America". Trev elaborated

"I know where it is, fuckturd!" Hector exploded like a bomb but without the shrapnel and horrendous injuries. "That's where I'm *from*. It's why I hired him at random out of the Chicago Detective Directory to follow my nemesis Devon Starbrood and find out where he's hiding Nefertiti's Eye, said to be worth priceless billions, which he stole from the ex-Nazi who runs Chicago Museum, who stole it from the sultan of Marrakesh in 1942, so it wouldn't really be stealing, I'd be bringing it back here, where it's from, and selling it to the Morroccans, cos I'm a good guy. But then I heard Starbrood found out Fritter was following him, and he was planning to get him and torture him to find out who he's working for, which would've spoiled my whole plan with the gemstone and all that, so, anyway, long story short, I needed to get to Fritter first and bump him off. Which is where *you* came in."

"Yes sir" said Trev. "I'm well aware this is a FAT operation"

"A fat *what*eration? interjected Maltoward

"A *Find-And-Terminate* operation sir" elaborated Trev

"Really, cos *so far,* it sounds like you're on a LAME operation, a *Lose-And-Make-Excuses* operation!" Maltoward growled impatiently.

"Actually, we think we've got him pretty much located now" said Trev .

"So, whereabouts he in Chicago Town then?"said Hector

"Well, we knew he was somewhere northwest of the lower east side-"

"Isn't everywhere?"

"Well, yes, if you're talking specifically about Chicago Town"

"Well where the freaking fuck else would I be specifically talking about? Jesus, what am I paying you turd-shagging shit-brains for!?!" chuckled Maltoward fondly.

"Point taken sir" said Trev "We didn't have much to go on as there had only been rumoured sightings, tantalizing glimpses, and breathless mumblings, so we started following Starbrood in the hope Fritter was following him too, cos that's what you originally hired him to do, and *bingo*, there he was, following him into a bar one night; so we sent in sexy decoy Agent G."

"Sexy dec- Oh, *Amy Gladly!* "Chirped Hector."Good old Amy. How is she, give her a big hug from me!" Said Hector.

"Er...please don't say agent's real names on the phone sir" [Author's note: Aha! So, that *was* her real name. I knew it!]

"Oops, I mean sexy decoy Agent G!" Said Hector

"So, what you up to now Trev, how's things?" he continued casually, then further-continued sinisterly: "And why isn't Jake Fritter dead?"

"Ok, again, let's try not to say people's names sir" said Trev patiently "With *Agent G* in situ we were-"

"Sorry, in whatu?" said Maltoward

"In situ sir; in place... in *The Target's* bachelor pad sir"

"Ok, gotcha, it just means in some place, ok, carry on."

"Thankyou sir. We were about to enter *The Target's* apartment"

"His situ"

"Er... yes, but he must have sensed us with some kind of

fifth sense, and he came out to investigate. Agent G followed him down and when he jumped outside in the prepared-to fight position, she knocked him out with a mallet disguised as a novelty mallet which she had had had secreted about her person.

We were about to bag him up and remove him in a bag-for-life-type-shopping-bag-but-bigger, when we were disturbed by the approachment of several police-cops, and were forced to quietly flee the scene and melt away into the foreboding shadows of the surrounding darkness with a mixture of relief and disgruntlement tempered by circumspection.

We then surreptitiously monitored the police-cop airwaves without them knowing, and traced *The Target's* whereabouts to the local hospital, but another woman took him out of there before our *pretend doctor* could enact *Plan B."*

"Pretend Doctor? Oh, Jeff Conroy, how *is* Jeff?" Said Hector, delighted at the mention of his old friend he grew up near. Jeff had always loved playing doctors and nurses as a child, and Hector was delighted to hear he'd finally gotten to play a real one, albeit pretend.

"Um, our *pretend doctor* is dead sir" said Trev, exasperated by all the name-mentioning,

"Oh, poor Jeff" says Hector, "I shall miss Jeff Conroy and his endless aimless anecdotes and bouts of non-infectious laughter. So, Fritter got away?"

"Yes sir, for now. The woman drove *The Target* to another apartment, presumably her own, where I secretly followed her to."

There was a long silence at the other end; a long, quiet, brooding, hideous, deadly, unfathomable and fairly banal silence.

"And?" said Maltoward finally, a single simple word, but containing a cold, sinister note of impatience, mainly in the "n".

"Oh, sorry, yeah, *and* now he's in this other woman's place, which we're outside now, and we're about to enact plan C." elaborated Trev

"Really? Interesting." mused Hector, making a note, without any pen or paper cos it was a mental note.

"Yes sir, I suppose it is really interesting." Says Trev, re-echoing Hector's sentiments back to him.

"No, I said 'Really, *question mark, new sentence, Interesting!*" corrected Hector, tersely. He liked to say things like *"Really? Interesting."* to make himself seem more mysterious and fiendish, but Trev had ruined it now. That made him terse, and he didn't like being terse, which made him terser.

"Kill him!" He snapped tersely. Two simple words, one of them lethal, the other primarily an indicator of gender.

"Kill him? Ok sir. Will that be all sir?" inquired Trev

"Yes, just kill him. Don't go beyond that." Said Maltoward "Oh, and Trev? Bring me back some Chicago Jam!"

"Jam sir?"

"Yes, that's still what Chicago's famous for isn't it?"

"I...don't know sir...I don't think so."

"Well, I've been away for a while; ok just bring me back a jar of whatever Chicago's famous for these days. You know where I am don't you, the Grand Hotel, 94 Fez Road, Marrakech?"

"No sir, I *don't* know that," Trev hissed in exasperation "(*I thought you wanted to keep your location secret sir!)*" he added emphatically in brackets.

"Oh yeah - ok, forget that. I'm not living anywhere in particular, like North Africa or anywhere like that, and certainly not in the main hotel in Marrakech, but come and find me, *wink wink.* Bye Trev!"

Hector Maltoward hung up, scratched his bright blonde fringe (the top front part of your hair that gets in the way of your eyes), took the sim card out of his phone, and melted it with his cigar, burning his left finger-you-point-with a bit and making him say *"Owww!"*

He took another hidden sim card from beneath the black band around his hat, and put it in his phone. But it wouldn't go in, it just kept popping out, and he had to use his fingernail to keep the card in till he put the little fiddly rubbery liddy kind of bit back on, and it was hard and pokey and it hurt his under-the-nail skin.

"Aaagh!" He said, or more colourful words to that effect, which you can imagine yourself, like fuck and cunt.

Then he sat back, sighing and tutting with a mixture of satisfaction and dissatisfaction, possibly faction?

CHAPTER 7

Sex-Frenzy

A t that moment, almost thousands of miles back the other way, Jake (on the couch) said to Sarah (at the window) "What do you mean, *'it might be a bit late'* "

"Actually, I said, *'I think we might be too late for that'* ", said Sarah

"Are you sure?" Jake implored querulously

"Certain", she said, "no need for querulous implorement".

Jake went over to the window, unsure whether his ex-girlfriend's cryptical words meant there was a baddie outside, or if was just a cynical ploy to get him to go over to her so she could kill him, or was it because she still had feelings for him, and she wanted to know what those feelings were, which would be easier to tell from close-up?

He went anyway, and they both looked out the window. For a second, he thought there was something moving behind the bushes, but it was probably just regular outsidey stuff. Anyway they were getting more interested in each other now than anything else anyway.

She edged towards him even more closer than what they already were, and he could smell his favourite lady-perfume that he'd got her for her birthday or Christmas or Valentines or Easter or his birthday, he couldn't remember, and he had no documentation on his person to verify the date. He knew he'd got it back in the day though, before she was his ex-girlfriend, when she was just his normal everyday girlfriend.

She felt his hot breath on her face cos he was breathing on it and the inside of his lungs was several degrees warmer than her face-skin, and all their pent-up feelings got unpented, releasing pheromones and sexual emotions, and the lust-link of their mutual past that they both had had had, flared up again, like one of those giant matches, you know the fireplace ones, and they started tearing off each-other's clothes like wild koalas in a sex-frenzy in the bargain bin of a clothes shop.

Her lips were everywhere, not just on her face but all over his body, and his hands were all over hers (her body, not her hands) and their legs were intertwined like platted hair, if you imagine flesh-coloured plats with knees. She pulled him into her, (not all of him, just his penis).

They made love in spasmodic spurts of unadulterated adult abandonment, interspersed with refreshment breaks and light reading.

Eventually, it was all over and they just lay there banjaxed on the floor, panting like labradors, in a heaving pile of two bodies, exhausted, not doing it anymore.

Was it good for you? he began to say, but before he got to the "r" in "for", Sarah's slidey-window-door shattered into loads and loads and loads of bits, and a tall skinny lanky thin lad with a gun sauntered in, tenderly brushing off the fragments of glass off of the sleeve off of his designer jacket. 'So, there *had* been something moving around behind the bushes', thought Jake, 'not just regular outsidey stuff!'

It was Trev. But Jake didn't know his name, because he'd never met him before and he wasn't wearing a "Trev" badge. Trev could've just opened the slidey-window-door, it wasn't locked or anything, but nobody had told *him* that, and they certainly weren't going to start now, with him waving a gun around and everything.

"Hello Jake", he said, " I'm here to kill you." Trev raised his gun up to the aiming-at-things position and started pulling on the trigger, his finger tightening inside the roundy hoopy bit of the gun where your finger goes.

"N-o-o-o-o-o-o-o" said Jake, in slow motion.

Before Trev could reply, the front door of the apartment shuddered with the impact of twelve bullets slamming through it, presumably from somewhere on the other side, at point blank range:

BAM, BAM, BA-BAM BAM BAM BAM BA-BAM BAM BA-BAM!

(Needless to say, whoever shot these bullets either had no thought for other people's safety, or worse, they were deliberately attempting to hurt or maim. Such actions, whether they be spontaneous and indiscriminate, or thoroughly and meticulously planned, are highly irresponsible, and any perpetrators should always be held to account and subjected to the most stringent of legal proceedings.)

The bullets narrowly missed everyone, except Trev, who got all twelve of them in him. He shuddered and jolted around like a puppet being violently puppeteered by a puppeteer having a spaz attack, as the bullets *thwacked, schlumped,* and *ffffwwted* into every major artery, heart and brain in his body. He spewed jets of blood like a man-shaped watering can full of blood that's been shot twelve times, and fell down as dead as a deceased lifeless slaughtered corpse of a body onto the floor.

Suddenly....BAM!!!BAM!!!BA-BAM!!!BAM!!!BAM!!!BAM!!!BA-BAM!!!BAM!!!BA-BAM!!!!!!! Came another, even louder volley from the other side of the door. (It was louder because the door was now bullet-riddled with holes and therefore no longer as sound-proof-worthy)

"Get down" Screamed Sarah! kicking Jake sideways as she hopped out of the way in the opposite direction. Jake gasped. He'd always admired her goatish nimbleness in the vicinity of ballistics, (though he'd never witnessed it, it was a kind of assumed admiration). The new bullets all also hit Trevor's lifeless body, making him flop and jerk around like a discarded doll in the back of a rickety van on a bumpy mountain road caught in an avalanche on an otherwise uneventful afternoon.

Before either of them could do anything, three masked men ambled in through the splintered doorway and kidnapped Sarah, shoving Jake rudely out of the way when he tried to intervene, which he did. Then, even quicker than they had arrived, which was moderately quickly, they were gone.

Jake looked forlornly at the place where Sarah had been, but she wasn't there anymore. It had happened, and that was that. Nothing could bring her back now, and there was no point going after the nasty baddies, because (a) they might shove him again, and (2) they were probably going faster than him, so he could never catch up with them anyway, it was a mathematical impossibility.

Anyway, there was a lot of tidying up to do, glass and blood everywhere, the lifeless deceased dead body of a slaughtered corpse, a broken door, you name it.

As he began Hoovering with the Dyson, Jake swore he would get her (Sarah) back; but how? He took out his phone to call the police-cops, and that gave him an idea of the one person that just might, or mightn't, be able to help.

CHAPTER 8

Klysnyvskyrz

The rain on the windscreen was like millions of diamonds that had been polished to roundyness, halved, then glued onto curved car-glass. Jake didn't care and wiped them off with a wipe of his wipers. He was driving like a madman who'd been let loose (without his regular mad-ication) in the front part of a car.

He drove over bridges and through tunnels, past pet-shops and playgrounds, along cobbled country lanes, across overpasses and along freeways. He broke several red lights, maybe more, and then, worried that everything was taking too long, he took a shortcut and skidded to a halt outside the police-cop station.

As the skid-dust settled around Sarah's Mitsubishi Lancer, (which luckily he'd found the keys to and knew how to drive), it revealed an old concrete window-pocked redbrick building; run-down, dilapidated and flea-riddled.

It reminded him of the buildings he'd seen in documentaries about buildings, except this one was full of police-cops. Living, breathing, fighting, jumping, yawning, sitting, typing, staring po-lice-cops. He went inside.

"Who you here to see?" said an elderly female police-cop woman behind the glass-fronted 'Hello' counter. With a gnarled bonsai (tiny japanese tree) hand, she flicked the dust off her huge signing-in book that visitors are meant to write their names down in.

She handed him a pen while he answered her. He didn't like doing two things at once, so first he signed, then he handed her the pen back, then answered, drawing himself up to his full height in feet and inches.

"Officer Klysnyvskyrz". He said, in his deep chiselled Chicago drawl. He was trying to sound casual, but deep down inside, he felt like this was one of the most urgent types of situation you could be in, like when you need to use the toilet but there's someone in there and you have to wait and someone else says why don't you go and pee in the lane round the back, but you can't cos it's a number 2, but you don't want to tell *them* that, cos they'll probably know 2 means a poo.

"And who might you be?" she said with one eyebrow raised and her lips curled into the lip section of a sarcastic expression.

"I *might be* Jake Fritter." he said, rebounding her attitude right back at her in return like a squashball from a squash tournament wall. At the mention of his name, the elderly old woman's curt grumpiness softened to gruff disinterest.

"I'll let him know you're here" she said, and then mumbled something mumbly on the phone to someone he couldn't see.

Minutes later, even though it seemed much longer, because the number of minutes was unspecified, she told him he could go in and go down the corridor and go left, take your first right after the photocopier, and it's the second door on the right, just past the mops and cleaning stuff, can't miss it.

"Thanks" he said, and he went that way and then he was there. He knocked gingerly, even though he was a brunette. Haha only joking. He just knocked moderately hard.

"Yes?" came a familiar voice. Jake went in and sat down.

"Well well well," said Officer Klym Klysnyvskyrz, looking up from his big old untidy police-cop desk "What can I do ya for?" which was his police-cop jokey way of saying "What can I do *for* you?"

Jake looked at his old friend's face; time had been good to

him, he had hardly changed.

"You still look the same as last week" Jake said.

"Look Jake", said Officer Klysnyvskyrz, "I don't have much time before my afternoon shift, so do me a favour, hurry up, get to the point, don't prevaricate, elaborate, or beat around the bush, keep it short and simple, just tell me why you're here, and tell me fast, no dilly-dallying, shilly-shallying, messing about or fumble-bumbling, and no time-wasters please."

Jake liked his old friend's expansive directness, and felt a warm glow of comradeship and chumly camaradery.

"Ok. I was with this woman and a guy came in and was about to shoot me-"

"Shoot you?"

"Well, he had a gun pointed in my general direction, and his finger was in the roundy bit where the trigger is"

"Ok. Sorry, we just have to be precise when we take statements, or else things get messy and people die."

"Somebody already has. This guy was about to shoot me and possibly the woman too, but then three other guys shot *him* through the door, and then they just barged in and took her without even asking, and now *she's* missing"

"Ok, describe her. First of all how old was she?" Enquired Klysnyvskryz

"I dunno, 20, 45 maybe"

Klysnyvskyrz's eyelids closed and vibrated a little.

"Ok...a woman... 20 to 45... I'm beginning to picture her in my mind's eye before I draw a sketch." Klysnyvskyrz took a pencil from behind his ear and began sketching in his notebook, which didn't have any lines in it, it was just plain which is less distracting and better for drawing. "Did she have any distinguishing features?" he asked.

"Distinguishing features? No, though she did have a kind of distinguished air, sorta haughty; here's a photo from when we used to be a thing".

"What kind of thing? Remember, we have to be precise or things get messy and people die"

"A couple thing."

Jake showed him a picture on his phone.

"Ah, now that's helpful. Good thing you showed me that. That's not how I pictured her at all". He scribbled out his stick-figure sketch and started again.

"The men took her away. I think she's been...kidnapped." Jake said, waiting for the shock to sink in, but it lingered somewhere between them, slowly dissolving. Then Klysnyvskyrz realized what Jake was saying, and it finally sank in.

"My god. *Kidnapped.* That's *awful.* You sure?" he quipped .

"Well they took her away and now I can't find her...so it doesn't look good. I tried to stop them but they shoved me. My arm got hurt."

"Oh you poor thing. Whereabouts?" the police cop inquired concernedly.

"Just here" said Jake, pointing to the bit between your elbow and your shoulder and wincing slightly. That's how sore it was, you couldn't even point at it.

"Shoving is so *rude!*" Klysnyvskyrz roared pensively.

"I know, right? People these days I suppose." said Jake resignedly.

"So they weren't nice men then?" Klysnyvskyrz scribbled a note in his notebook.

"No, in fact they were quite gruff" responded Jake

"Ok, I'll prepare a bulletin." He (Klysnyvskyrz) began writing on a form "A man has been killed. A woman has been kidnapped. Another man has been shoved. Kidnappers described as gruff."He looked up. "Any more other different details I need to know?"

"No, not that I can think of. Oh...hang on, oh yeah, there was *another* woman who disappeared a few hours before that, at my place, after I was knocked out by persons unknown. The police-cops said there was no-one else there when they got there just in time after noticing my blinds were drawn slightly differently than usual, so *she* might've been kidnapped too." said Jake

"Ok, I'll change that to 2 women", Klysnyvskyrz tutted, harrumphing as he corrected the statement. He changed the initial "A" of the sentence for a "2" and the "a" in woman for an "e" to make it "women". It looked a bit messy with the corrections, but it would have to do. Now it read: "A man has been killed. 2 women has disappeared. Another man has been shoved."

"Any photos of her?" barked Klysnyvskyrz quietly

"Yeah, I just showed you" Jake responded

"No the *other* woman, the first one." Klysnyvskyrz pressed

"The first one I talked about?" Jake parried

"No, the *second* one you talked about, the *first* one that disappeared!" Klysnyvskyrz countered

"Oh, Amy! No, I'd only just met her; I usually wait a few weeks before I ask them to pose for a photo, for which I charge very reasonable competitive rates." said Jake.
Klysnyvskyrz nodded and began to sketch fast and hard, like a police-cop possessed.

"Did she look like this?" he said finally, after signing and dating the sketch

"That's amazing" Jake said, "you're very good at drawing."

"Thanks" says Klysnyvskyrz, "it's a Ford Mondeo."

"Yeah, king of cars. But she wasn't a car, she was a woman, the king of women." Jake's eyes began misting up with a mixture of soft melancholia, light fog, and mawkish desire. Klysnyvskyrz scribbled a bit more on the picture

"Now who's time-wasting?" said Jake, getting impatient and shifting impatiently in his seat to show his impatience.

"Now, look again", says Klysnyvskyrz, "at the woman inside, driving the Mondeo. Is *that* her?"
Jake marvelled at the detail of the sketch. The chrome lining around the car's windows was slightly tarnished here and there with spots of rust and a few hairline cracks, and the windows themselves were sepia-tinted glass with a slight marbled sheen of overnight frosting.

There was a dazzling prismatic spectrum-slash of sunshine across them, but you could just make out a long-haired shadow inside. It did kind of look like her, he thought, but it was hard to tell. It could be just an ape in a wig.

"I'm not sure," he squinted "I...can't really make her out."

"Well, at least we've got something to go on. I'll put an APB bulletin out on all points, and a warning on local media.

"And then what?" said Jake

"And then, we wait. " said Klysnyvskyrz

"And then what?" said Jake

"And then...hey, do you want a game of pool?" Said Klysnyvskyrz with a mixture of excitement, rage and glee.

"Do I!?!" Said Jake, "Do bears defecate primarily in heavily forested temperate and sub-arctic zones!?!"

They began playing virtual pool against each other on Klysnyvskyrz's iPad till suddenly the phone rang:

Briiiiinnng!!! Briiiiinnng!!! Briiiiinnng!!!.. Briiingg!!! Briiiinnggg!!!!!. Briiiiinnng!!!.. Briiingg!!!!...Briiiiinnng!!!.. Briiingg!!!... Briiiinnggg!!!!!. Briiiiinnng!!!!..Briiingg!!!!... Briiiinnggg!!!! Briiiiinnng!!!.. Briiingg!!!!...

Klysnyvskyrz answered. "Yeah? You sure? I'll be right over." He grabbed his jacket and stood up.

Jake wished he'd had heard the other side of the conversation

"Is it... a lead?" He enquired tentatively, trying to hide his excitement

"Even better", said Klysnyvskryz, not trying to hide *his* excitement at all. It was written all over his face, *italicised* with delight and <u>underlined</u> by a big grin "It's lunchtime. Sandwiches!"

CHAPTER 9

Starbrood

Sarah was in a dingy basement, about 3 miles away, give or take a kilometer. A voice was talking to her.

"Optimism, from the Greek *opti* meaning 'to see', and the Welsh *miasma*, meaning mist or blurredy-ness. So, *optimism* translates as 'To see unclearly' My own interpretation, but one I think you'll agree is of considerable merit".

Sarah tried to turn her gorgeous award-winning oval-shaped face towards the direction the voice was coming from on her left, but it wasn't easy, what with her voluptuous supermodel body tied to a chair and a combination of scarves, gaffer tape, and daisy chains tied around her head to something wooden behind her, probably a chair, keeping her front part of her face, except her eyes, from moving. The mysterious voice continued from where it had been talking from.

"So you see, Sarah Fluzzblunter, if that is your real name-"

"It is." She muffled, through her scarf-gaffer-daisy combo gag. She was lying, it wasn't really. Her real name was Vixen-schnauzer, but whoever owned that carefree, convivial voice was probably a baddie, if her recent kidnapping, imprisonment and past experience of carefree conviviality was anything to go by, so she wasn't going to tell *him* that. "And I don't see how your defin-ition of optimism is markedly different from the original, other than in nuance!"

"Good point, cogent and well made! Well then, let me put it this way," the voice re-continued again, "I would venture that you are being a trifle *optimistic*, in our re-appraised but broadly unchanged sense of the word, about your prospect of escaping your current predicament."

"Oh fuck off" she blurted, tired of his casual but haughty demeanour.

"Well may you blurt", he said, "but it is unwarranted blurtage. History is littered with such blurts-" he began to elaborate, paraphrasing various utterances blurted by famous figures throughout history, a collection of untimely expostulations, unexpected interjections, unheralded interruptions and other impetuous enunciations. Then, in the midst of his unsolicited elucidation, without warning, a warning emitted from the radio in the corner.

"Warning," a police-cop voice crackled "A man has been killed. Two women has been kidnapped. Another man has been shoved. The kidnappers are armed and gruff. If you see the women or their kidnappers please contact the coincidental - excuse me, I mean *confidential* number, available on request, which will connect you to the emergency services, which will gauge your level of priority, activate pertinent procedures should they be deemed necessary, and put you through to the next available member of our automated service personnell. Please hold. Your call is important to us. Thankyou for your time"

The as-yet unidentified kidnap-boss lunged at the radio, trying to switch it off before the message could be heard, but he was slow at lunging, and had only got halfway there by the time the message was finished.

Then, just as the man was returning to his original position which was sitting over there, the warning re-commenced again. "If you see anyone who looks suspicious, do not approach them as they may actually *be* suspicious, as well as extremely dangerous and possibly violent. If you spot the kidnappage victims Sarah Vixenschnauzer and Amy Gladly, *do* approach them though, as they are harmless enough and probably need your help; but do be careful, it may be a trap! Actually, *don't* approach them, just in case, you never know. Obviously, if you feel you absolutely have to whatever you do do, *do*."

"So, your name isn't Fluzzblunter after all. "Said the mastermind of her kidnap. "I must admit I had my suspicions, as there is no Fluzzblunter in any phonebook, online directory or other contact service anywhere; it's not even a name, you just made it up, I just checked, so there!"

He loomed into view, and Amy could at last see him for once. He was a tall loomy type, with a long chin and sapphire-brown eyes which seemed to twinkle with a mixture of murderous intent and normal reflected room-light. He had average hands and a jacket, and he sported a copiously bushy black moustache which would have looked sinister on anyone else, but on him, was bland and inconsequential. His head-hair was light brown.

"Hang on, where's my manners? Allow me to introduce myself" said the man "I am Devon Starbrood".

Sarah was shocked by the mention of the name, feared throughout the world of High Finance, International Banking, and Criminal Skullduggery. Suddenly it all clicked, like one of those clickers you click for training dogs. She realised *this* was the D.S. Jake had been on about. Then she remembered hearing something about Starbrood running Chicago's biggest criminal syndicate until he decided to go *legit* and used his dirty money to buy himself a clean job managing the World Bank, but while he was the World Bank Manager he got done for fraud or embezzlement or maybe both, fraudbezzlement? She couldn't remember, she'd only heard it from some kid going past her on a bike in the park, and the last thing he said before he spun away round the bend was that Starbrood was back running Chicago's underworld again.

"And you, I believe, are Sarah Vixenschnauzer? Judging by your ID card." He held out her ID card for her to look at.

"Hello Sarah. Do you mind if I call you Sarah? Would that be ok? Would you have any problem with that? Is that alright?"

No response. Sarah's beautiful, critically acclaimed lips remained as silent as the lips on the mouth of a mute statue that can't speak cos it's made of inanimate statue-stuff.

"Hello? Sarah? Do you mind if I call you Sarah?" He tried again. Finally he gave up, like a *loser*.

They sat in silence for what seemed like hours, but was actually 3 minutes less.

"Water" said Sarah finally."I need water"

"Ah yes" he mused, pouring a glass and holding it up to the intense light of the interrogation-lamp, which he'd got in Ikea, once he'd found his way out of the three-hundred acre maze of the lighting department "Water, the water of life. Some call it the water of the gods."

He brought it over and moved the gag in her mouth to where you'd have a moustache if you were a man, (but she wasn't, she was every bit a woman, and then some, believe me!) He held the glass of water out for her to drink, as she couldn't do it herself with her own hands cos they were tied to the chair, thanks to him, or no thanks to him, depending on how you look at it. She took a sip and spat it out, ruining his trousers.

"Not *still* water! *Sparkling!!!*" she demanded.

"Oh sorry, er, ok." He went embarrassedly back to the fridge and refilled the glass with fizzy water while she tutted audibly, wondering what his bloody problem was. He raised the glass to her lips again. This time she drank loads of it, until the glass was empty, and it was a *big* glass, about the size of a medium glass but bigger.

"Anyway, I've been following your progress, even while your *ex* has been following mine"

"What?" She said, suddenly intrigued even though she was trying to act all casual and disinterested like she didn't even care.

"Didn't you know? your friend Jake Fritter, PI had been hired by my arch enemy and sworn nemesis Hector Maltoward, to follow me around.

'Oh my God, and that's the H.M Jake mentioned!' she thought, 'Jake was right, this really *does* go all the way to the top.' She vaguely remembered hearing how Maltoward, a cobbler by trade and a poet by passion, took over Starbrood's illegal cobbling and poetry operations when Starbrood went legit, and quickly expanded to run the whole Chicago underworld, but then Starbrood got sacked from the World Bank for fraudbezzlement and came back. They were about to go to war, but then Starbrood cleverly used his I.M.F connections to get Maltoward a seat on the U.N in Morrocco, and they both cooled off on the war thing, or something like that. She wasn't sure, the kid who told her *that* was on a skateboard going the other way while she was still processing what the kid on the bike'd said.

Starbrood continued, unaware of her cogitations.

"You see, Maltoward wasn't happy sitting on his gold-plated balcony in Marrakesh, he wanted a certain sapphire, said to be worth priceless billions which I had *expropriated* from the estate of Hans Knopfler, the ex Nazi war-criminal and who runs Chicago Museum, and is also the dad of that bloke in Dire Straits. *Knopfler* had pillaged the sapphire from a Morroccan sultan during Rommel's North African rampage, so I wasn't really stealing, I'm a good guy.

Anyway, I don't particularly like being followed around, so I had *Jake* followed around by my mate *Tim*, who got on Jake's trail while *he* was following *me*, and I lured him to a bar where he started laughing with some woman, but then Tim turned around to scratch an itch on his back. I'm always telling him there's no point turning round to scratch your back, cos your back will always just be behind you, and you'll have to keep turning round for ever, but by the time he realised this and turned *back* around, Jake and the woman were gone.

The trail went cold, colder than an ice lolly in a freezer-truck stuck in a snowdrift in the ice age. Damn, thought Tim, and began to feel morose and dejected, wondering if there was any point doing anything, if life itself, in the ultimate analysis, is essentially meaningless.

But then, with a flash of inspiration out of nowhere, he realised Jake may have simply left the bar with the woman, and so Tim went outside and *bingo!* There they were, right in front of him, so the trail warmed right up and got hot again, hotter than a freshly-lit industrial welding-torch dropped into the erupting spout of a super-volcano.

When Jake and the woman got to his condo, Tim, who had been following them on his motorbike, which was specially muffled for following people silently, soon realized he wasn't the only one following Jake. He noticed, also following at a discreet distance on the other side of the street, Trev.

Trev used to work for me as occasional henchman and part-time dogs-body. I know what you're thinking, do I only hire people with one-syllable T-names? But it's just a coincidence, honestly! Anyway, a few weeks ago, Trev left to work for only marginally better pay (and not as good holidays), as a full-time minion for Maltoward. (I know what you're thinking, if I'm *Jake's* nemesis and Maltoward's *my* nemesis, shouldn't that make *him* Jake's friend? But no, it doesn't work like that, us nemesises all just hate each other and everyone else, pity that's how it is, but what can you do?)

So anyway, Tim spotted Trev, and luckily Trev hadn't seen Tim, but Tim didn't want to get in his way, cos he knew Trev was a notorious hitman, and Tim wasn't going to risk his neck for anyone, I hadn't hired him after all, he was just a mate, doing me a favour, fair play to him!

Anyhoo, Tim hung around a while longer unnoticed in the foreboding shadows in the undergrowth in the background on his motorbike, and he saw the whole thing: Jake coming out of the slidey window door things, whatever they're called, then the woman he was with comes out behind him and knocks him out with some kind of novelty mallet, then she starts talking to Trev, and Tim realises *she* must be working *with* Trev, for *Maltoward*. Anyway, they're about to bag Jake up in a bag like one of those bag-for-life shopping bags only bigger, when suddenly the police-cops turn up just in time, but it's getting dark, you know that kind of dusk light, so their visibility is low visibility, and they don't see Trev and the woman, who slink off into the shadows like slinks -

"Sorry, I zoned out" Sarah said, "what were you saying?"

"Er, ok... where did you drift off? Anyway, doesn't matter, Tim told me what had happened, so I listened to the police-cop airwaves, which led me to the hospital, and then *you* hooked up with Fritter in the hospital. *Bango!*

I just had to wait till you came out with Fritter and follow you to where you went and then send in my three masked amigos (not Mexicans, or even friends, just people I hired) Tom, Todd, and Tobe, (I know, with the T-names again, right?)

They love to shoot things, especially if the things are people. And I was happy to let them shoot Jake, but only after they'd brought him to me for interrogation. Anyway, they got a bit over-zealous, shall we say, and ended up shooting *Trev* by accident a few dozen times, and in all the excitement and confusion they lost their instructions which I'd given them on a scrap of paper, and grabbed *you* instead of Jake! Id*iots* or what?

Anyway, I'm telling you too much, and hey, why am I open-ing up to you? I guess you just seem like the kind of person I can talk to, but let's hear *your* story. In particular, where's Jake? I sent them back in to get him later but he was gone, you wouldn't hap-pen to know where would you? No? Well, let me tell you some-thing else..."

Sarah, who had a short attention span, nodded off, and when she woke up he was still going on. "...which is why there's so much dark matter in the universe... but I digress. It really is time for *you* to talk now. I've told you far too much already, so I'm afraid I can't really let you live, apologies in advance, nothing per-sonal, but before I relieve you of your last living breath, I just need to know one thing. Where's Jake?"

Sarah just stared at Starbrood blankly, blinking occasion-ally.

"OK." said Starbrood eventually, breaking the trance "I'll just go and get a few little things that might help you remember. Memory aids, you might say"

He got up and limped out of the room (most of his left leg had been blown off in Vietnam; only the foot remained).

By craning her ears and listening intently, she could hear him sharpening a selection of blades and drillbits in the next room. That didn't sound very nice, and she wished her hearing was a bit shitter. She also wished she wasn't so securely tied to the chair, and banged her fist on her knee in frustration. Then she looked at her fist in growing wonderment, burgeoning appreciation, and expanding excitement. Her fist, and indeed everything else about her left hand, was free!

He had had had her right hand tied to the chair with a secure reef-knot, but'd only used a regular bow-knot on her left hand; what an idiot! She quickly loosened the bonds around her head and neck, and looked around, noting all possible escape routes, which was none. Bum*mer!*

She was just starting to try and untie the reef-knot on her right hand, when Devon Starbrood limped back in with a tray full of gleaming implements of painful persuasion.

CHAPTER 10

Ghosts

"Mmm...these are damn good sandwiches!" Exclaimed Jake

"I know, right?" said Klysnyvskyrz, "That's why I've stayed in the same job all these years. The number of times I've been offered promotions which'd take me to another precinct with more fulfilling work, or a pay-rise to move to a different department and/or building which didn't include access to these sandwiches... I just *couldn't!*"

This conversation was muffled by sandwich munching, so this is really only a guess at what they were saying, but an educated one.

"What I don't get is why someone would want to kidnap Sarah? I mean, what's she ever done to anyone?" Said Jake, probably; it was hard to tell with all the sandwich-muffling.

"Maybe she murdered someone and they wanted to murder her back?" suggested Klysnyvskyrz.

"Yeah but if they were murdered they'd be dead, so how could they?" said Jake

"Hmm, good point, unless it was *a ghost!*" mused Klysnyvskyrz

"How long have you been a police-cop detective?" inquired Jake

"Hah… More years than I care to remember, but definitely less than nine." said Klysnyvskyrz

"And how many of your cases turned out to be done by a ghost?" pressed Jake

"Let me see…I've worked on quite a few. Hmmm…Yeah, none actually. Ok, so we can rule out ghosts. Which leaves….we're getting close, I can feel it!" Said Klysnyvskyrz, his eyes growing wild with excitement.

Then they went out in Klysnyvskyrz's police-cop car with the siren wailing and the blue lights spinning and flashing like in a police-cop movie, and drove around looking for clues.

'So, this must be what it feels like to be an undercover police-cop' thought Jake. Then he saw something that made his heart stop. Or at least that's what it felt like, cos that'd've been fatal. It was just an ordinary lull between beats and then it began beating again and he sighed with relief, but nevertheless he was overcome with shock by what he'd seen that'd originally made him think his heart'd stopped in the first place.

CHAPTER 11

Death Masks

Outside the basement door, Sarah ran up the concrete stairs to the tradesman's entrance, which was at street-level, and vaulted over a spiked railing onto the street, which was also at street level. Behind her, the gate on the spiked railing swung open in the wet Chicago wind. She could've just walked through it, but she didn't know it was unlocked when she vaulted over it; she didn't even know it was a gate, she just thought it was a railing with no gate, but it was one of those ones that're like half the railing long, and they only have a tiny bolt and teeny-weeny hidden hinges, so they just look like a fixed railing without a gate, so that's why she didn't just open it; plus she was in a bit of a hurry, so you can't blame her. If you still blame her, it says more about you than her.

She ran and ran and ran, and kept running. Then she ran some more. The soft Chicago rain gently pounded down on her beautiful worried face like water falling out of the sky.

She reached the corner, or as they say in America *the inter-section between blocks* at the end of the street, stepped out onto the boulevard and started running across the avenue, and suddenly BAM-BAM-BAM! she ran straight into the 3 masked men who had originally abducted her and who Devon Starbrood had only minutes ago alerted to go and find her and get her back after she had surprised him with a blow upside the head with her free left hand and then untied her other hand while he was temporarily unconscious, but then he came round and lunged at her with his tray of implements, but he was still groggy and slow at lunging and she kicked him in the nuts'n'guts with a twirling two-footer and ran out the door.

Todd, Tom and Tobe had got the call from Starbrood on their way back from a game of darts (Tom won, Todd lost, Tobe did the scoring thing with the chalk, which kept breaking, which made everyone a bit narky, plus he wasn't very good at subtracting. He'd done ok with addition in school but never really got the hang of subtraction.

It was something he was quite sensitive about it, but he hid both his sensitivity and his arithmetic ineptitude quite well, and had even taught advanced mathematics in Stamford University for several years, until someone asked him to take 7 from 23. He faked a stomach cramp and ran to the toilet, but was confronted by his faculty superiors the next day.

He left Stamford under a cloud of gossip, rumour, and incredulity, his piercing intellect now blunted and in question, but still sharp enough to hack his way through a forest of raised eyebrows with an undergrowth of wagging tongues... but I digress.

Anyway, the three lads were on the way back when they got the call from Starbrood, and then they literally bumped into Sarah. At first, they started saying stuff like "Oops sorry, excuse me", kind of thing, but when they realised this was the very Sarah Vixenschnauzer they just been told to recapture, their tone changed from profusely apologetic to deadly sinister, with a cold cynical edge and a frisson of melancholia.

They all raised their guns together simultaneously at the same time to her beautiful award-winning head, threatening to make a centrally-intersecting triple bullet-tunnel in her worried but beautiful brain.

"Ha, got you!" They said, taking a word each, but forgetting to do it sequentially, so it came out as "You-Ha-Got!". Their eyes seemed to flash with a cold blue light as they began to squeeze their respective triggers. Then Sarah realized their eyes *were* flashing with a cold blue light: police-cop light!

CHAPTER 12

Retinas

Klysnyvskyrz's police-cop car had been swerving down the avenue with lights blaring and sirens blazing and while he was trying to stop it the brakes failed in the slidey-rain conditions, and totally out of control, his police-cop car ran over the three baddies, *BUMPETY-BUMPETY-BUMPET!* and nearly also ran Sarah over, luckily skidding to a just-in-time halt.

Jake and Klysnyvskyrz jumped out and they all said hi. Jake hugged Sarah with all his might and she hugged him back with reasonable force. He said "Are you ok? We were *soooooo* worried!"

"I'm fine" said Sarah, "I was incarcerated by this one-legged two-footed freak round the corner, who just kept going on and *on*, and then he was gonna torture me but I sucker-punched him upside the head and two-footed him in the nuts-n-guts and escaped."

"Oops, sorry, where's my manners!" Said Jake, "Sarah Vixenschnauzer this is Officer Klym Klysnyvskyrz, Klysnyvskyrz this is Vixenschnauzer, the woman I told you about."

"I know" said Klysnyvskyrz, "your description fits perfectly, "she's a woman, 20 to 45, with hair."

Klysnyvskyrz took Sarah's huge hand, did a slight bow and kissed the back of it, like something out of Dangerous Liasons, if they have that in America.

They heard some groans and looked under the car at the 3

masked minions who were unrecognizably mangled and dead or dying. Klysnyvskyrz reversed the car off them and they all bent down and they each cradled one of the dead or dying men's heads in their respective hands.

"Who sent you?" said Klysnyvskyrz, but his one was dead (won't bother with names as they were unrecognizably mangled). Sarah repeated the question to her one but his head had been flattened by the impact so it was more like a frisbee, with his mouth as the outer rim of the frisbee, and try as he might, he couldn't talk.

Finally, Jake questioned his lad, who just looked normal (his face had been unrecognizably mangled into another, normal-looking face), "Who sent you?" he said, and his one replied "Devon Starbrood, he wanted to get one up on Hector Maltoward, you know the way it is."

Then the light started to go out of his eyes, and they began to close for the last time. Then the light came back in them and they opened again and he said to Jake: "By the way, sorry we shoved you, I know it was rude, but we were in a bit of a hurry"

"It's OK" lied Jake bravely, "It was a bit sore at first but it's ok now" he pointed to the slight bruise on his arm, which had been fading and was now gone.

But the light had gone out of the guy's eyes again and then they closed forever cos he now was totally dead, his body and vital organs and nervous system had had had enough, and he died screaming peacefully in Jake's arms.

Suddenly, the air was full of more sirens, blue lights, helicopters and police-cops, as the whole Chicago police-cop force seemed to, and indeed did, descend on the scene and cordon it off with police-cop crime-scene cordon-tape, and made everyone move along, saying "Move along now, nothing to see here, move along, go on, move along, nothing to see, move along now..."

Jake dropped his fella's dead head on the ground, and stood up, his manly, tear-filled eyes flashing blue with all the police-cop lights. He gently led the dazed, stunned and traumatized, but still achingly beautiful Sarah, away from the carnage that lay all around them, and they went over to an unfolded fold-up alu-minium-and-plastic table outside a roadside café on the sidewalk pavement and sat down in post-traumatic shock.

Klysnyvskyrz, shuffling and jiggling with involuntary crash-tremors, followed them over. He flipped open his iPad and showed them the live long-distance feed on his InterPol App which normal people can't get, only police-cops. It was helmet-cam video of Hector Maltoward, everyone's nemesis, being ar-rested and subdued by a Navy Seal SWAT team who'd been heli-copter-roped onto his hotel balcony in Marrakech, acting on in-formation from the Chicago wing of the C.I.A, who unbeknownst to anybody except themselves, had bugged Trev's phone with a bug, and used Hector's ill-advised unguarded name-and-place-specific communications to track him down and get him.

Meanwhile, with his other hand, Klysnyvskyrz held out a pocket mirror from out of his pocket which he angled to line it up with several-dozen other mirrors and lenses of various sizes and angular alignments dotted over rooftops, chimneys and lamp-posts in the area, in a three dimensional multi-periscopular array, which showed what was happening in a house only a few blocks away.

Through the shaky mirror in Klysnyvskyrz's shuddering trauma-tremored hand, they saw that Devon Starbrood, every-one's *other* nemesis, was being arrested and subdued in the middle of enjoying a live web-feed of an off-off-broadway all-female stage version of "Twelve Angry Men" on his laptop, which he'd started watching after he called Tom, Todd, and Tobe, may they R.I.P.

The F.B.I. had had had a bug on Starbrood's landline for years and planned to arrest him next month for multiple crimes going back years, when they had enough evidence for a water-tight case, but'd been forced to act now cos of the C.I.A moving in on Maltoward, and they didn't want the C.I.A to get all the glory.

Publicly, the C.I.A and F.B.I said they had been working together all along, in a kind of F.B.C.I.A joint operation, but in pri-vate reality, it was just cos neither one wanted to lose the limelight to the other one, kind of like Maltoward and Starbrood in a way, except more governmenty and agenty.

The F.B.I. agents told Starbrood to fetch the priceless gemstone, and he looked around a bit, but couldn't find it and couldn't remember where he'd put it. They said "Are you sure?" and he said "Yeah" and they said "Hmm well...ok then", and they took him away.

Jake couldn't help noticing, even though the mirror was shuddery, that in the background of Starbrood's kitchen, peering out of a wicker basket full of clothes marked "to be washed", was the unmistakable upper face (nose, eyes and fringe) of Amy Gladly, undetected by the F.B.I. guys.

She was watching it all happen but not saying anything cos then she'd've been caught. Jake didn't say anything either. Something held him back, he didn't know what, maybe it was his emotions. So, *Amy* had double-crossed him and knocked him out with whatever she hit him with, he thought, realizing now it was probably her novelty mallet, which must've been an *actual* mallet just *disguised* as a novelty mallet! *Duh!*

And it must've been Amy with Trev in the bushes outside Sarah's place which he'd just thought was regular outsidey stuff. Trev was only *half* the outsidey stuff, Amy was ther other half! And she must've followed Sarah when *she* got kidnapped, to find out where Starbrood was, and then snuck in to try and rob Nefertiti's eye, said to worth priceless billions, for herself!

So Amy had double-crossed him *and* Trev *and* Maltoward, *and* Tobe'n'Todd'nTom, *and* Starbrood, or at least some of all those. Well, he had to admire her cunningness, in a way. But to think he'd doubted Sarah who he knew for years, when it was *Amy*, who he'd just met and trusted completely (like a stupid dumbass lovestruck imbecilic *asshole*), who'd been the danger all along! Just goes to show, you should never trust people you trust and always trust people you don't.

Tired of it all, Jake gently-but-firmly pushed away Klysnyvskyrz's hand-mirror, and firmly-but-gently closed the faux-plastic cover on his iPad, not wanting to see any more. Klysnyvskyrz smirked understandingly, and went back to helping the other po-lice-cops with the mess he'd made.

Jake took Sarah by one of her huge hands, and they stood up, as police-cop and forensics activity swirled around them and those fellas with the crime-scene tape went mad running yellow tape around everything.

They looked deep into each other's eyes; really deep, past their corneas, beyond their irises, through their pupils, lenses, and vitreous chambers, right back to the dense webbed network of veins on their respective retinas.

She knew it was him, Jake Fritter she still wanted, and he knew, at last, that it was her, Sarah Vixenschnauzer he truly trusted and loved, not Amy Gladly, who he now knew was a cold treacherous vixen hiding in a basket somewhere anyway, so she was pretty much unavailable.

Together, Jake and Sarah, hand in big hand, walked off into the dry, humid, moonless, pitch-dark, neon-drenched flashing blue Chicago night together with each other.

In Sarah's other (probably just as big) hand, she clenched something hard and heavy, something which every now and then, sparkled with the same blue light as the police-cop lights all around them, except that this object's blue light came from within its insides, as it still glowed with the love with which the renegade pharaoh Akhenaten had imbued it with when he gifted this sapphire, said to be worth priceless billions, on his deathbed, to his beautiful sorceress wife Nefertiti all those years ago, and which she had then cursed should it ever leave her possession: Nefertiti's Eye. (Not her actual eye, it was just called that.)

The End

ABOUT THE AUTHOR

Saul Tillock is an avid amateur topiarist and world-renowned author, writer and typist, specializing in murder mystery crime suspense thriller fiction and all other types of fiction as well. His works have been translated over into countless numbers of languages, including American, Australian, Canadian, Binary, and New Zealian. He teaches creative writing in Harvard, normal writing in MIT, joined-up writing in Trinity College, and wood-work in the Dublin Institute of Technology. He lives in Dublin with his dogs. (He used to have two dogs but one ran out on the road because he never shut the door properly when people called in and they said you should watch those dog cos they'll keep running out and one day one'of'em'll get killed, but he just laughed, till one day the dogs ran out and one got knocked down and died. A car was involved, and a neighbour, who was in the car at the time, was driving. The neighbour was very apologetic, so Tillock said ok, but he knew deep down it was completely the neighbour's fault, or his own, at least one of them was to blame. He felt quite bad about it for a while, but eventually, he moved on with his life and got another dog to go with the one that was left).

Printed in Poland
by Amazon Fulfillment
Poland Sp. z o.o., Wrocław

60599697R00035